THE RUGRATS FILES
A TIME TRAVEL ADVENTURE

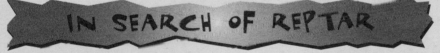

IN SEARCH OF REPTAR

The Rugrats Files

A Time Travel Adventure Series

A TIME TRAVEL ADVENTURE

IN SEARCH OF REPTAR

by Steven Banks
illustrated by the Artful Doodlers

SCHOLASTIC INC.

New York Toronto London Auckland Sydney
Mexico City New Delhi Hong Kong Buenos Aires

KLASKY
CSUPO INC.

Based on the TV series *Rugrats®* created by Arlene Klasky, Gabor Csupo, and Paul Germain as seen on Nickelodeon®

ISBN 0-439-40583-1

12 11 10 9 8 7 6 5 4 3 2 1   2 3 4 5 6 7/0

Printed in the U.S.A.

First Scholastic printing, September 2002

CHAPTER 1

Two enormous dinosaurs with sharp-looking teeth stared down at Tommy Pickles and Chuckie Finster.

"Look at those big ole dinosaurs!" cried Tommy.

"D-D-Do I have to?" asked Chuckie nervously. "Let's get out of here, Tommy. We're sir-rounded!"

The dinosaurs were close enough to touch, and that was *exactly* what Tommy wanted to do. He slowly reached out his hand.

"Tommy, don't!" cried Chuckie, grabbing Tommy's hand. "Your daddy said 'Don't touch the dinosaurs!'"

Tommy and Chuckie were at the Natural History Museum. They were looking up at skeletons of a brontosaurus and a stegosaurus. The room was filled with giant dinosaur bones and fossils. There were even dinosaurs painted on the walls.

Tommy's dad, Stu, had come to the museum to do some research for the Reptarland theme park in France. The company that ran Reptarland wanted him to design a new ride called "Dancing Dinosaur."

"I just can't figure out how dinosaurs would have danced," Stu said to his wife, Didi. "I don't understand how they supported their big bodies with those little feet, much less how they moved around. Maybe I can figure it out by looking at the skeletons."

Didi had come along to the museum and brought Tommy, Chuckie, Kimi, Phil, and Lil with her. "It'll be an educational field trip," she said. "Dr. Lipschitz's new book says that museums are good for developing minds."

While Stu and Didi looked at the map of the museum, the babies crawled over to another dinosaur skeleton.

"C-C-Can we go home now?" asked Chuckie. "They gots scary stuffs at this mooseum."

"You don't have to be afraid, Chuckie," said Phil. "It's just a skellyton."

"Skellytons is just bones," added Lil. "Like after you eated fried chicken."

"But they're *real* bones," said Chuckie. "And they used to be *real* scary dinosaurs!"

"I wish I could see a real live dinosaur," said Tommy.

"Me too," said Kimi.

Chuckie shook his head. "Not me. If I ever got close to a real live dinosaur, I'd run away as fast as I could!"

A tour guide walked by, leading a group of tourists. She pointed down the hall. "If you follow me, ladies and gentlemen, we will see our most popular exhibit—a complete skeleton of a Tyrannosaurus rex."

"They must call him that cuz he wrecks everything," Lil whispered to Phil.

"C'mon, kids, let's join the tour," said Didi as she followed the tour guide. When they got to the T. rex room, the babies had to lean way back and crane their necks to see the gigantic skeleton. Didi put on a headset that played a recording of information about the Tyrannosaurus rex.

"He looks just like Reptar!" said Chuckie.

"Except he's not wearing any skin," added Tommy.

The tour guide continued. "The words 'Tyrannosaurus rex' are Greek. They mean 'tyrant king.'"

"He doesn't look like a tired king to me," said Lil. "He looks like a mean one."

"If he's a king, how come he don't gots a crown on?" asked Phil.

The babies crawled closer to get a better look.

"I wonder if he's Reptar's great-great-great-grandfather," said Chuckie. "Do you think he'd like to see my new Reptar toy? I gots it in my Smiley Meal yesterday."

Tommy held out his hand, "I wanna see it, Chuckie."

"It was real hard to get. Me and my daddy waited in line for a long time. It's a collectible," said Chuckie. "Now I gots all twenty Smiley Meal Reptars. Every single one. The whole collection. It's got a super dino-grip and it makes a growly noise when you squeeze its tummy."

"But all the Reptars they give away in Smiley Meals gots dino-grip and make the growly noise," said Kimi.

"But this one is . . . *red!*" said Chuckie.

"You gots the red one!" exclaimed Tommy. "I never ever seen a red one. You're so lucky, Chuckie."

Chuckie nodded and patted his pocket. "I gots it right here. Safe and sound."

"Let's see it!" said Tommy.

"Okay, but be real careful," said Chuckie.

He reached his hand down into his pocket and felt around. Nothing. He reached into his other pocket. It was empty too. Chuckie couldn't remember if he brought it with him. Did he leave it in the car? Was it still at home? Or worse, could it have been Reptar-napped?

CHAPTER 2

"Reptar's gone!" cried Chuckie.

Tommy put his hand on Chuckie's shoulder. "Don't worry, we'll find your Reptar."

"No, we won't. I losted him," said Chuckie sadly. "I'm always losing stuffs. I'll never see Reptar again."

"You can go get another Smiley Meal with a new Reptar toy, Chuckie," said Kimi.

Chuckie sniffled, "No, I can't. I gots the last one on the last day they gave them out. They're giving away a Dactar toy now."

Lil held up her half-eaten candy bar.

"You wants the rest of my Reptar candy, Chuckie?"

Chuckie shook his head. He didn't want candy. He wanted his new toy back.

Just then Stu walked up. "Okay, kids. Time to go home. Hope you all had a good time."

Didi took off her headset. "Did you figure out how dinosaurs would have danced?" she asked.

Stu shook his head. "Not yet. This one's a real brain-buster. I'll have to do some more work at home."

"But it's Saturday, Stu," said Didi. "I thought we were going to take the kids to Buck E. Bee's for dinner?"

"I know, Deed, but this is important," said Stu. "If I can't find out how to make the dancing dinosaur ride, I'm going to be in trouble with the folks at Reptarland."

Tommy leaned in close to his friends.

"Did you guys hear that? My daddy is going to be in trouble if he doesn't figure out how to make the dinosaurs dance!"

Chuckie sulked the whole car ride to Tommy's house. When they arrived, Grandpa Lou was there baby-sitting for Dil.

"You've got to buy a new chair!" he demanded.

"What's the matter with this one?" asked Stu. "You love this chair."

"Not anymore!" said Grandpa Lou. "There's a broken spring or something poking me in my you-know-what!"

"Let me take a look at it," said Stu.

Grandpa Lou stood up. There was a red toy on the seat—it was Chuckie's Reptar!

Chuckie gasped. What if Grandpa Lou had squished it and it didn't roar anymore?

"That's what's been giving you your problem, Dad," Stu laughed. "It's Chuckie's Reptar."

"His *what*-tar?" asked Grandpa Lou.

"His little toy dinosaur," said Stu. "He left it on your chair." Stu picked it up and handed it to Chuckie. Chuckie immediately tried the dino-grip and then squeezed the stomach. It let out a roar. Chuckie sighed in relief.

Grandpa Lou sat back down in the chair. "That feels much better! So, where have you and the sprouts been, Stu?"

"We took them to the Natural History Museum. They saw the dinosaur exhibit," said Stu.

"Dinosaurs, eh?" said Grandpa Lou. "Did you see the skeletons? The great big ones? The T. rex?"

"Yup. They saw it all," said Stu. "I have to make an important call to Reptarland in Paris before they close for the day. Can you watch the kids?"

"I can watch *anything*," Grandpa Lou said with a nod. "Anything at all . . . except golf tournaments."

"Thanks, Dad," said Stu as he trotted off to his office.

Tommy, Chuckie, Kimi, Phil, and Lil looked at Grandpa Lou.

"I always liked dinosaurs," he said. "Pretty amazing creatures. Didja know they lived *millions* of years ago?"

Chuckie whispered to Tommy, "Did Grandpa Lou play with dinosaurs when he was little?"

"Maybe," said Tommy. "He's pretty old."

Just then Angelica, Tommy's older cousin, came in carrying her Superstar Cynthia doll. "What's everybody talking about?" she demanded.

"Dinosaurs," said Grandpa Lou. "I'm telling the sprouts all about 'em."

"I know *everything* about dinosaurs," said Angelica.

"Stick around, and you might learn a thing or two," said Grandpa Lou. "Some dinosaurs were as big as buildings, and some were as small as chickens. The strangest thing about dinosaurs is that they disappeared over sixty million years ago, and nobody's sure why. All of a sudden—*Poof!*—they were gone! Extinct!"

Tommy nudged Chuckie and whispered, "Maybe somebody did a magic trick and gots them to disappear."

Grandpa Lou leaned in close. "Some scientists think the dinosaurs died because an asteroid hit the earth. KA-BOOM!"

"My daddy had an asteroid," said Angelica. "He went to the doctor and got it fixed."

Grandpa Lou continued. "The asteroid

was so big, and it hit the Earth so hard that it sent up a cloud of dust that was big enough to block the sun."

"My mommy puts sun blocks on me so I don't turn into a lobster," Angelica interrupted again.

Grandpa Lou cleared his throat. "If you stop interrupting me, missy, I can continue."

Angelica shrugged. "Go ahead."

"Then it got so cold that all the plants stopped growing and died," Grandpa Lou said. "And the dinosaurs that ate the plants didn't have anything to eat, so they all died too. And then the dinosaurs that ate the dinosaurs that ate plants had nothing to eat after awhile either. So they all died."

Chuckie looked at Grandpa Lou wide-eyed.

Grandpa Lou shifted in his chair. "Another idea the scientists have is that

a star exploded up in space and gave off radiation, and the earth got *real* cold. Freezing! Dinosaurs were too big to hibernate in caves like bears, and they didn't have feathers or fur to keep them warm, so they couldn't survive the cold weather." Grandpa Lou stretched and yawned. "The one thing we do know for sure is that the dinosaurs disappeared. They're all gone . . . no more . . . so long . . . kaput." He yawned again. "Adios . . . sayonara . . . kicked the bucket . . . went to the great dinosaur ranch in the sky . . ."

Grandpa Lou's eyes closed and his chin fell to his chest. Then he started to snore.

"Look! Grandpa Lou's hibernating," said Tommy.

"He sure knows lots about dinosaurs," said Kimi.

"You babies are so gullible," said Angelica standing up. "I know the *real*

20

reason dinosaurs are egg-stink. Grandpa Lou couldn't tell you the truth 'cause you're just dumb babies and you'd be too scared."

"Tell us, Angelica," said Tommy.

"I can't," said Angelica. "It's a deep, dark secret. Only a few special people—like *me*—know about it. Sorry, babies!" And then she walked out the door to the backyard.

Tommy followed after Angelica. He called to the others, "C'mon, guys, we gots to find out the dinosaur secret!"

CHAPTER 3

Tommy's dog, Spike, was taking a nap in the backyard. He lazily opened one eye to look at the babies and then shut it again.

"C'mon, Angelica!" pleaded Tommy. "Tell us!"

"I'm too busy right now," said Angelica as she smoothed the hair of her Cynthia doll. "What do you wanna play now, Cynthia? Queen Angelica? Angelica Superstar? The Legend of Angelica the Great?"

"Please, Angelica!" begged Tommy. "Tell us about dinosaurs! Then maybe I can help my daddy find out about those dancing dinosaurs—"

"And we can get to go to Buck E. Bee's to eat!" said Phil.

Angelica sighed and put Cynthia down. "Well, okay. But don't tell anyone else."

The babies gathered around Angelica. She got a serious expression on her face and then spoke quietly. "Dinosaurs came from . . . *outer space*."

"Outer space!" exclaimed Tommy. "I knew it!"

"Shh! It's a secret," said Angelica. "You see, dinosaurs lived in outer space on their own planet."

"What planet?" asked Tommy. "Was it Mars?"

"Was it Poopeter?" asked Phil.

"Or Venice?" asked Kimi.

"Stop guessing and I'll tell you!" said Angelica. "It was called the planet of the dinosaurs."

"I've never heard of that planet," said Tommy.

"And you're not *gonna* hear about it if you keep innerruptin' me!" said Angelica.

"All the dinosaurs lived on the planet of the dinosaurs. It was way out in space about a gazillion miles," Angelica continued. "On the planet of the dinosaurs the sky was purple and the water was pink. The dinosaurs had jobs and lived in houses and drove cars. All the little dinosaurs went to dinosaur school. And one day the dinosaur explorer, Columbosaurus, discovered the planet Earth."

"Did he use a tellyscope?" asked Lil.

Angelica narrowed her eyes. "The dinosaurs wanted to go to Earth for a vacation 'cause they were tired of working and going to school, so they built a rocket ship. When they got to Earth, they went swimming in the ocean and had beach parties and stuff. But when they wanted to go back home, this evil guy wrecked their rocket ship and put them in a zoo. So they had to build a new rocket ship out of trash and stuff, and that took a zillion years. But they finally did it, and they all went back to the planet of the dinosaurs and lived happily ever after."

"Is that what really happened?" asked Kimi.

"Of course it is!" said Angelica. "I saw it in the movie *Return to the Planet of the Dinosaurs, Part Two*."

"That's not true," cried a voice from behind the fence.

Everyone turned to see Susie Carmichael, Tommy's next-door neighbor, skipping into the backyard. She was the same age as Angelica, but Susie knew a lot more about a whole bunch of different things.

Angelica glared at Susie. "What do you mean it's not true?"

"I belong to the National Geological Dinosaur Club," Susie said as she pulled out a little white card from her pants pocket. It had a picture of a dinosaur on it and Susie's name, too.

"Just cuz you got a card with a dinosaur on it doesn't mean you're a dinosaur expert," said Angelica.

Then Susie pulled out a rolled-up magazine from her back pocket. There was a picture of a dinosaur skeleton on the cover. "I get a dinosaur magazine every month with all sorts of facts and pictures. My mom reads it to me."

Everyone crowded around to look at the magazine except Angelica.

"'Dinosaur' is a Greek word," said Susie. "It means 'terrible lizard.'"

"I like lizards," said Phil. "They're delicious."

"Especially slimy ones!" agreed Lil.

"Dinosaurs aren't lizards," said Susie.

"But some of them *were* terrible."

"I don't like terrible dinosaurs," said Chuckie. "But I like Reptar." He held up his Reptar toy and squeezed its stomach. *Roar!*

Nearby, Spike raised his head and barked. Then he jumped up and trotted over. He snatched Reptar out of Chuckie's hand! The toy dangled from Spike's mouth as he ran away.

"Hey!" yelled Chuckie. "Spike just stole my Reptar!"

"He didn't steal it, Chuckie, he just borrowed it," said Tommy. "We're opposed to share."

"Ew!" complained Chuckie. "He's getting doggie juice all over it!"

"He just wants to play fetch," said Tommy as he walked over to Spike. But Spike ran into the bushes and disappeared.

"Spike wants to play hide-and-seek!" said Phil.

Everybody ran into the bushes . . . except Chuckie. Chuckie didn't want to play games. He just wanted his Reptar back.

"C'mon, Chuckie!" called Tommy.

Chuckie didn't move. "I don't know, Tommy, it looks pretty dark in there," he said. "And those bushes look real itchy and scratchy, and there might be bugs. . . ."

Tommy stuck his head out of the bushes. "You wanna get your special red Reptar back, don't you?"

"Well, um, yeah. I guess," said Chuckie.

"C'mon, then!" said Tommy as he held a branch back so Chuckie could go in. "I'll be right with you the whole time."

Chuckie took a deep breath and crawled into the bushes.

CHAPTER 4

The bushes *were* dark and scratchy. The babies had to duck and twist and turn to get through. The branches scratched their arms, and leaves tickled their faces when they brushed up against them. Chuckie saw bugs everywhere he looked.

"I don't like bushes one bit," said Chuckie, just as a cricket landed in his hair. "Ahhh!"

"Shh, Chuckie!" said Tommy. "I think I hear something."

A strange noise echoed in the distance. It was getting louder and louder. A strong smell filled the air.

"Where are you, Spike?!" Tommy called out. "Hey, guys, I think I see something!"

"Is it good or bad?" asked Chuckie nervously.

"It's amazing!" said Tommy.

Angelica pushed her way to the front. "This better be good!" she said. "I didn't come all the way through those itchy bushes to see some dumb . . ." Angelica's jaw dropped.

Tommy, Chuckie, Kimi, Susie, Phil, and Lil were standing at the edge of a lake. The sun sparkled on top of the water, and a soft breeze blew. There were big green trees and strange plants they had never seen before. Way off in the distance was a tall mountain with smoke coming out of the top.

"I have a feeling we're not in my backyard anymore," said Tommy.

"This looks just like the pictures in my

dinosaur magazine!" cried Susie.

"Susie, do you think we'll see any dinosaurs?" asked Tommy. "We could help my daddy figure out how to make the dancin' dinosaur ride for Reptarland!"

"I don't think dinosaurs danced," said Susie. "And besides, they didn't have any music."

"They had music in *Return to the Planet of the Dinosaurs, Part Two*," scoffed Angelica.

"Where are we?" asked Kimi.

"I don't know, but I think we better go home," said Chuckie, heading back to the bushes. "C'mon, Kimi!"

Chuckie grabbed Kimi's hand and started to lead her away.

"I don't wanna go back, Chuckie," said Kimi, pulling her hand loose. "I wanna see all this neat stuff."

"Doesn't anybody wanna go back to the nice, safe backyard?" asked Chuckie.

Everybody shook their heads. Chuckie stared down at the dirt. He wished he wasn't so scared.

"Spike! Spike!" yelled Tommy. "Spike, c'mere!"

The babies looked around, but no one could see Spike. They looked under bushes and in hollow logs and behind big rocks, but no Spike.

"Maybe he went back through the bushes," suggested Chuckie. "Maybe he's in the backyard. I'll go check."

Tommy grabbed Chuckie's hand. "Doncha wanna find your Reptar toy?"

Chuckie thought about it for a moment. The red Reptar was the centerpiece of his collection. He looked up and nodded reluctantly.

"And we have to find Spike, too," said Tommy.

"Okay, let's go," said Chuckie. "But let's make it quick."

Just then they heard a loud noise in the distance. It sounded like a roar.

"W-W-What was that?" asked Chuckie.

"It must be Spike," said Tommy. "He's prob'ly barkin' at a bird or something."

The noise got louder and the ground started to shake.

"I gots a very bad feeling about this!" said Chuckie.

Leaves started falling off the trees. The water in the lake started to ripple.

"Look! The water's dancing!" said Lil.

"Something's coming, and I don't think it's Spike!" cried Chuckie.

CHAPTER 5

The babies couldn't believe their eyes when they saw a real living and breathing and *very* large dinosaur coming over the hill. He was as tall as a building and had four giant legs as wide as tree trunks. His long tail came to a point at the end. The dinosaur had a neck as long as a giraffe's and a tiny little head on top. It slowly walked up to the lake.

"A real live dinosaur!" cried Tommy.

"I wish he was just a skellyton like in the mooseum," said Chuckie.

"It's a brachiosaurus!" exclaimed Susie.

"Oh, poor backy-o-sore," said Lil.

"Does that mean his backy is sore?"

"No. Brachiosaurus is his name," said Susie.

"I knew that," said Angelica, even though she didn't.

"He's the biggest dinosaur there was," said Susie. "Eighty feet tall. He weighs as much as fifty elephants!"

As the dinosaur came closer Chuckie yelled, "We're all gonna be dinosaur dinner!"

"Don't worry, Chuckie, he won't hurt us," said Susie confidently.

"How do you know?" asked Angelica. "Are you a dinosaur mind reader?"

"Because he's a plant-eater," said Susie.

"He's a veggie-narian," said Phil.

"Does he take care of animals?" asked Lil.

Angelica rolled her eyes. "It means he doesn't eat meat, bald brain."

The brachiosaurus walked up to the lake, dipped his head to the water, and took a long drink.

"Looks like he's a water-eater," said Chuckie. "And that's fine by me."

The brachiosaurus drank for a while, then raised his long neck and started nibbling leaves from the top of a tree.

"I sure wish Grandpa Lou was here to see this," said Tommy.

Suddenly a dark shadow crossed over them as something flew over their heads.

"Look! Up in the sky!" cried Tommy.

"It's a bird!" yelled Phil.

"It's a train!" shouted Lil.

"It's a dimorphodon," said Susie.

"A what?" asked Angelica.

"Dimorphodon. You say it like 'die-more-foe-don,'" explained Susie.

"It looks like a flying dinosaur," said Kimi.

The dimorphodon circled high over their heads. The strange-looking creature had wings that were five feet from tip to tip. It had a big head, sharp teeth, and even sharper claws. The babies watched as the creature circled above them.

"Uh . . . Susie . . . what does a di-moron eat?" asked Phil.

Susie looked up nervously. "Oh, he's a meat-eater."

"I don't want to see any me-eaters, you guys!" said Chuckie, and he covered his eyes.

The dimorphodon flew across the lake and then disappeared over a hill.

"Whew!" said Chuckie. "That was a close one."

The babies turned back to see the brachiosaurus still eating. Almost all of the leaves on the tree were gone.

Tommy laughed. "He's giving the tree a haircut!"

"He sure is hungry," said Chuckie as his stomach rumbled.

"He has to eat a lot of food 'cause he's so big," said Susie.

"I'm hungry too," said Kimi rubbing her stomach. "Breakfast feels like a million years ago."

"I could eats two peanuts-butter-and-jellyfish sanditches," said Lil.

"Well, if we can figure out how dinosaurs would have danced, my daddy won't have to work, and he can take us to Buck E. Bee's!" said Tommy.

"Yeah, well I'm hungry now!" said Angelica. "Did any of you babies bring any snacks?"

They all shook their heads. "Honest, Angelica," said Tommy, "we don't gots anything."

"Empty your pockets!" demanded Angelica. "Up against that rock and spread 'em!"

The babies turned around and leaned their hands against a big rock. Angelica frisked them for treats.

Tommy giggled, "That tickles, Angelica!"

"You're clean," she said. Then she felt something in Phil's shirt pocket. "What do we have here? You been holdin' out on us, Mr. DeVille?!"

"I forgots I had it," said Phil. "What is it?"

Angelica pulled out an old, soggy, brown banana from Phil's pocket. "Yuck!" she screamed.

"Maybe we can eat leaves," suggested Lil as she looked up at the brachiosaurus. "He sure likes 'em!"

Angelica crossed her arms. "I'm not eating leaves! I'm not a dinosaur."

"We can find food later," said Tommy. "First we gotta find Spike. And I'm gonna get some help." He walked right toward the brachiosaurus.

"Tommy, what are you doing?!" shouted Angelica. "Are you bananas?!"

The closer Tommy got to the dinosaur, the bigger it looked and the smaller Tommy felt. Quick as a flash the brachiosaurus darted his head to the ground to get a close-up look at Tommy. Tommy was face-to-face with the dinosaur.

"Tommy!" yelled Chuckie. "Nooooooo!"

CHAPTER 6

"Hey, Mr. Dinosaur!" yelled Tommy. "Have you seen my dog, Spike?"

The brachiosaurus looked at Tommy curiously and then returned to eating the leaves at the top of the tree.

Tommy yelled again, louder, "We gots to find him, Mr. Dinosaur! Spike's my best doggie, and he gots my friend Chuckie's new Reptar toy, and we wanna get it back!"

The brachiosaurus paid no attention to Tommy.

Susie walked up beside Tommy. "He can't understand you."

"Can he understand you?" asked

Tommy. "Do you speak Dinosaur?"

Susie laughed. "No. I don't speak Dinosaur."

"Ah-ha! So you're *not* the big dinosaur expert you said you were," crowed Angelica. "You can't even talk to a dinosaur!"

Susie sighed. "Nobody can talk to a dinosaur. Dinosaurs can't talk."

"But they talk on TB," said Tommy.

"Yeah, and they talk in *Return to the Planet of the Dinosaurs, Part Two*," said Angelica. "They even sing!"

"Those aren't real dinosaurs," said Susie. "They're pretend."

Angelica ignored Susie and kept talking. "My favorite song is 'We're Going Back to the Place We Long to Be.' I know all the words. They sing it right near the end of the movie, when all the dinosaurs are about to break out of the zoo and fly back home in their spaceship."

"You're not going to sing it now, are you?" asked Susie.

"What a great idea!" said Angelica.

"We're goin' back to the place we long to be.
That pretty, pink planet in a far-off galaxy.
So let's take a little trip
On our homemade rocket ship,
And go back to the place
That puts a smile on your face.
So grab your favorite dinosaur and—"

"WOOF! WOOF!"

Angelica stopped singing. "Don't innerrupt me!"

"What was that?" asked Phil.

"It's another dinosaur!" cried Chuckie. "And he sounds mean, and he sounds like he's going to eat us!"

"Hey, that's no dinosaur," Tommy said. "That's Spike!"

"WOOF! WOOF!"

The sound was coming from the other side of the hill.

"He sounds close," said Susie. "Let's go find him!"

Tommy started to run. "We're gonna get your Reptar back, Chuckie! C'mon!"

Everybody ran off toward the sound of Spike barking—except Angelica, who kept on singing.

"Hey! Where are you going?" Angelica shouted. "Come back here! I'm not finished!"

Tommy, Chuckie, Kimi, Phil, Lil, and Susie disappeared over the hill.

Angelica shook her head. "You can't inspect dumb babies to appreciate talent!" She sat down on a rock. "Well, I'm gonna wait right here till they come back. I'm not gonna go chase some stupid dog for some stupid toy."

Suddenly it got very quiet. Angelica

looked around at the eerie prehistoric landscape. Something moved in the bushes. Then she heard something scamper behind her. Angelica hopped up and ran to catch up with the babies. "Hey! Wait for me!"

CHAPTER 7

"WOOF! WOOF!"

"Don't worry, Spike!" yelled Tommy. "We're comin' to get you!"

Tommy led the way as they crawled over stumps, ducked under branches, and climbed over a big tree that had fallen down. Angelica caught up with them as they waded across a shallow stream.

"WOOF! WOOF!"

They crawled through a small space under a giant rock that was wedged between two smaller ones. It was dark and damp. The dirt was cool on their hands and knees as they scurried along.

"Keep crawling!" commanded Tommy.

Spike's bark got louder. As they crawled out into the bright sunlight they saw Spike. Chuckie's Reptar was clenched in his mouth. And right next to Spike was the biggest egg they had ever seen. It was as tall as Angelica and twice as wide.

"Who laid *that* egg?" said Angelica.

"There must be a pretty big chicken around here," said Tommy as he petted Spike, who happily licked his face.

"I don't want to meet that chicken," said Chuckie.

"A chicken didn't lay that egg," said Susie, looking around carefully.

Phil ran up to the egg and sniffed it with his nose. "I bet it's a candy egg! Filled with chocolate!"

"Or marsh-meadows!" said Lil.

"I don't care what it is!" said Angelica. "I'm hungry and I'm gonna crack it open and eat it!"

Susie grabbed Angelica's arm just as Angelica was about to karate chop the egg. "I wouldn't do that if I were you."

Angelica yanked her arm free. "Well, you're not me and that's unlucky for you. Outta my way, babies! I've got an egg to crack! Egg cracker coming through!" Angelica climbed on top of the egg and stood up. She raised her arm over her head and was just about to smack it down on the egg when she heard a rumbling sound.

CRACK.

Angelica looked down and saw a teeny-tiny, itsy-bitsy crack in the egg.

CRACK. CRACK.

"It's opening all by itself!" said Lil.

The egg started rocking back and forth. Angelica frantically waved her arms around trying to keep her balance. She wobbled back and forth as the egg rocked and tipped.

"Jump, Angelica!" yelled Tommy. "NOW!"

Angelica jumped off the egg just as a spiked tail pierced the crack.

"Sumpin' inside that egg wants to get out!" cried Chuckie. "And I don't think we should wait to find out!"

A piece of eggshell fell off, and a mouth and two eyes appeared. Then a head popped out.

"It's a baby stegosaurus!" said Susie.

"I was just gonna say that," said Angelica. "But I don't like to show off."

The baby stegosaurus cracked open another piece of the shell. He got his front legs out first and then struggled to get the rest of himself out by shaking back and forth.

"Should we help him get out?" asked Tommy.

Susie shook her head. "No. He'll make it."

"I'm glad I didn't come out of an egg," said Chuckie. "That looks like a lotta work. It's much easier when the stork brings ya."

The baby stegosaurus tried to walk, but his legs were wobbly. He fell down the first few times, then he stood up and looked around. He had stubby little legs and a short tail with spikes on it. Even though he was a baby, he was as large as a cow.

"That's the biggest baby I've ever seen!" said Angelica.

"We could ride him like a horsey," said Kimi.

"No, thanks," said Chuckie. "I got a better idea. Let's go home."

Tommy shook his head. "That baby got born today. We gotta sing 'Happy Birthday' to him."

"I am not wasting my beautiful voice on that ugly creepture," said Angelica.

"I think he's cute," said Susie. "I wonder where his mommy is."

Spike began to sniff the baby stegosaurus. Then the baby stegosaurus started to sniff Spike. They went around and around in circles sniffing each other, and Spike dropped Chuckie's Reptar toy out of his mouth.

"You better get your Reptar before that baby dinosaur steps on it, Chuckie," said Tommy.

Chuckie carefully reached down and picked up his Reptar. It was all wet and sticky. As Chuckie began to shake off the slobber the stegosaurus looked up and trotted toward Chuckie. Suddenly the baby stegosaurus leaned in and snatched the Reptar toy from Chuckie's hand with his mouth.

"That baby ate my Reptar!" shouted Chuckie.

The baby stegosaurus took off running

with Chuckie's toy. Spike chased close behind, and the two of them disappeared over a hill.

Chuckie threw his hands into the air. "Here we go again!"

CHAPTER 8

The babies followed Spike and the baby stegosaurus up over the hill. The sun was beating down and there wasn't very much shade. The babies were tired and thirsty.

"I'm so thirsty I could eat a horse," said Phil.

When they came around a big rock they saw a small lake in the distance.

"Water!" cried Tommy. And they ran toward the lake.

"Last one in's a rotten leg!" yelled Lil.

Just as they got to the edge of the lake Susie yelled, "STOP!"

They all stopped short just at the

edge. Susie sniffed the air with her nose. She smelled something strange. It was a bad smell. A really bad smell.

Angelica held her nose. "Do one of you stinkin' babies need a new diaper?"

Phil and Lil checked their diapers.

"Not me," said Lil.

"Clean as a thistle!" announced Phil.

"It's the water that smells," said Susie. She bent down to get a closer look. The water was black and thick.

"It's a stinky mud lake!" said Lil excitedly.

"Let's take a stinky mud bath!" cried Phil.

They both took off their matching shirts and were about to jump in when Susie stopped them.

"That's not mud," said Susie. "It's tar!"

"What's tar?" asked Kimi.

Susie thought for a moment. "Well, it's kinda like the oil they put in cars, but it's a lot thicker and stickier."

Phil stuck his little finger into the water. "It's sticky!" he said. "Let's take a stinky, sticky tar bath!"

Susie shook her head. "That's not a good idea. Dinosaurs used to get trapped in tar pits like this. They thought it was water, and they would come down for a drink or to cool off. Then they'd get stuck in the tar and couldn't get out."

Angelica was still holding her nose. "Can we please get away from this stinky stuff?"

"Look!" shouted Tommy. "There's Spike and the baby dinosaur!"

"And he's still got my Reptar!" said Chuckie.

Spike and the baby stegosaurus were on the other side of the lake. Spike was curled up under a tree, taking a nap. The baby stegosaurus had dropped Chuckie's toy near the edge of the lake and was walking toward the black water.

"Oh, no!" said Susie. "He's going into the water! He's gonna get trapped!"

"Don't do it, baby dinosaur!" yelled Tommy.

Susie started running toward the dinosaur. "Quick! We've got to stop him!"

But it was too late. The baby stegosaurus walked farther and farther into the black tar. Then he stopped moving. He tried to lift his legs, but they were stuck. He tried to turn around, but he couldn't.

"He can't get out!" cried Kimi.

The baby stegosaurus began to whimper and make a strange calling noise.

"A baby's gotta do what a baby's gotta do," announced Tommy. "We gots to help him!"

CHAPTER 9

"Chuckie, you find a long stick," said Tommy. "Then the dinosaur can grab it and pull himself out."

Susie shook her head. "He can't grab anything. He doesn't have hands."

"Too bad he doesn't have dino-grip like Reptar," said Chuckie, cradling his toy.

Tommy paced back and forth. "I wish we had a crane. Or a tow truck."

"Or a bridge," said Susie.

"That's it!" said Tommy. "We can be a bridge!"

"Be a bridge? Tommy Pickles, you are bananas!" said Angelica. "That is the dumbest idea I've ever heard!"

"Do you have a plan, Angelica?" asked Susie.

Angelica glared. "Not yet. But when I do, it'll be a zillion times better than Tommy's or yours!"

Tommy walked over to a big tree that had fallen into the lake. It almost reached where the baby stegosaurus was stuck in the tar. "If we all hold hands, I bet we could reach him. Then we could pull him out together," said Tommy.

The baby stegosaurus was struggling to get out of the tar pit. But the more he struggled, the more he got stuck.

"You think it will work?" asked Susie.

"It gots to!" said Tommy. "Everybody, follow me."

Just then Angelica stepped forward. "If you wanna do something right, you gotta do it *my* way! I'm in charge of this operation. All you babies, up on that tree trunk! Move it!" she barked.

The babies climbed onto the fallen tree that went across the lake. Angelica stood on the edge of the water and watched.

"Aren't you going to help pull the dinosaur out, Angelica?" asked Susie.

"Of course I'm going to help," said Angelica. "I'm gonna stay right here and make sure you and those crybabies don't mess things up."

Susie shook her head and climbed onto the trunk. Tommy was at the end of the tree, closest to the baby stegosaurus. Kimi was behind Tommy, and behind her were Phil, Lil, Chuckie, and Susie.

"Grab hands!" bellowed Angelica from the shore. They joined hands in a line across the tree.

Tommy reached his hand out to the baby stegosaurus.

"I'm almost there!" shouted Tommy.

"A little, itty bit farther! I can almost grab him!"

The baby stegosaurus stretched his neck out toward Tommy.

"Don't worry, baby dinosaur, we're gonna help you," said Tommy as he hugged the dinosaur around the neck and pulled.

"I gots him! Don't let go!" ordered Tommy. "Now, everybody get ready to pull!"

"Pull on *three*," shouted Angelica. "One, two—"

"Three!" yelled Susie.

They all pulled. The baby stegosaurus didn't move. He began whimpering loudly.

"He's not coming out!" cried Chuckie.

"Pull harder!" yelled Tommy. "Pull as hard as you can!"

Then the baby stegosaurus started to move a little bit.

"Keep pulling!" shouted Susie.

The dinosaur slowly found his grip on the trunk and pulled himself out of the tar. The babies crawled off the tree and back to the shore.

"We did it!" yelled Tommy.

The baby stegosaurus was covered with black tar, and he didn't smell very good, but he was safe. He leaned forward and licked Tommy's face with his big wet tongue.

"Ew!" said Angelica. "That's worse than getting kissed by a frog!"

"You saved him, Tommy," said Susie.

"Excuse me?" said Angelica. "Who was in charge? Who gave the orders?"

"We all saved him," said Tommy. "Now let's get Spike!"

"And get out of here," added Chuckie.

"I don't think so," said Susie, looking over Angelica's shoulder.

Angelica put her hands on her hips

and narrowed her eyes. "And why not?"

"Because," Susie whispered. "The baby stegosaurus's mommy is behind you, and she doesn't look happy!"

The babies slowly turned around. There, on the other side of the lake, was a large stegosaurus. She had big, flat plates along the top of her back. She had a tail like the baby, but with much bigger spikes. She was low to the ground and had a little head.

"W-W-What do we do?" asked Chuckie.

"Let's move away from her baby," said Susie. "Very slowly."

As they quietly backed away Chuckie whispered to Susie, "Is she a me-eater or a veggie-table eater?"

"Vegetable," said Susie.

"Whew," said Chuckie, wiping his forehead with his hand, "I was just about to start worrying."

"You can still worry, Chuckie," said

Susie. "We helped her baby, but she might think we were trying to hurt it."

"What's she gonna do?" asked Kimi.

Susie gulped. "I don't know. But my mommy would be pretty mad if she thought someone was trying to hurt me."

The mother stegosaurus stared at the babies. Her eyes narrowed and she made a strange grunting noise.

"W-W-What was that?" stammered Chuckie.

"Sounded like a strange grunting noise to me," said Angelica.

Then the mother stegosaurus started to move toward them.

"Get ready to run," said Tommy.

But just as the mother stegosaurus reached the babies, she turned and walked over to the baby stegosaurus.

"I bet she's going to see if he gots a boo-boo," said Chuckie.

"The stegosaurus is a really neat

dinosaur," said Susie. "See those bony plates sticking up on her back? That keeps her cool. When she gets hot, the heat goes up out of those. And the spikes on her tail protect her from enemies. Her head is low and close to the ground so she can eat plants."

"I hope she doesn't think we're plants," said Chuckie. "What if she thinks my hair looks like carrots?"

After sniffing the baby stegosaurus, the mother turned and looked at the babies.

"That's the way my mommy looks at us when we make a mess in the kitchen," said Lil. Phil nodded.

"We're doomed!" cried Chuckie.

"I gots a plan," whispered Tommy.

"What is it?" asked Susie.

Tommy shouted, "RUUUNNN!"

CHAPTER 10

The babies ran away as fast as they could, and Spike followed. But so did the mother stegosaurus with her baby trotting behind her.

Susie looked back over her shoulder. "Don't worry, stegosauruses can't run very fast," she said. "Their legs are too short."

"So are ours!" cried Chuckie.

The stegosaurus was closing in on them fast. They ran around a big tree and hid, but the dinosaur kept coming. They ran and hid behind a big rock. But the dinosaur still found them. There was nowhere to go. They were trapped. The mother stegosaurus was standing less than ten feet away, staring right at them.

"Maybe she's gonna thank us for saving her baby?" wondered Tommy.

"I don't think so," said Susie.

"Don't worry. Any minute the dinosaur rocket ship is gonna come and take all the dinosaurs away," said Angelica. "Any minute now . . ."

"I wish the real Reptar was here," said Chuckie. "He would save us."

"Pipe down, Finster!" Angelica cried. "If it wasn't for you and your stupid Reptar, we wouldn't be in all this trouble!" She stomped her feet and waved her arms in the air. "Spike wouldn't have taken that dumb toy, and we wouldn't have had to come here and get chased by a crazy dinosaur!" she yelled.

Suddenly Kimi pointed. "Hey! Look! The mommy's going away!"

They couldn't believe their eyes. The

mother stegosaurus had turned around and was running away with her baby trotting behind her.

"What happened?" asked Tommy.

"I think Angelica scared her away," said Susie.

"Thanks, Angelica," said Kimi.

"I didn't scare anybody away! I'm not scary!" Angelica hollered. "I'm just mis-understood."

"Can we PLEASE go home now?" begged Chuckie. "I gots my toy and we found Spike and we don't need to stay here anymore."

Tommy put his arm around Chuckie, "Okay, Chuckie. That sounds like a good idea. Let's go home!"

A big grin spread across Chuckie's face.

And then they heard a roar from behind them.

Chuckie's grin disappeared. "That

doesn't sound so good," he said. "Not good at all."

A huge, dark shadow passed overhead. Something was behind them. Something big. The babies slowly turned and looked up . . . and up . . . and up . . . and up . . .

CHAPTER 11

"IT'S REPTAR!" shouted Chuckie.

Standing on top of a rock, looming over them, stood an enormous Tyrannosaurus rex. All forty feet of him. He had a big head and sharp, pointy teeth. The T. rex, not Angelica, had scared the stegosaurus away.

The babies stood frozen with fear. The T. rex moved along the edge of the rock and knocked down a small tree. The tree rolled right down next to the babies, and they dove behind it to hide.

Chuckie peeked over the tree. "Hi, Reptar," he whispered, sounding a little unsure. "I-I-I knew you'd save us."

"Shhh!" hissed Angelica as she put her hand over Chuckie's mouth. "That's not Reptar!"

"That's a real T. rex," whispered Susie. "And we don't want him to know we're here."

"What does this one eat, Susie?" asked Kimi.

"Anything he wants," said Susie. "He's a meat-eater. He's *king* of the meat-eaters."

They all huddled behind the tree as the tyrannosaurus stood above them. Chuckie looked up at the huge dinosaur and forced a smile.

"Aren't you scared, Chuckie?" asked Tommy.

"Nope," said Chuckie. "He's one of Reptar's cousins. He won't hurt us."

"I don't think he's seen us, so we're safe for now," said Susie.

"Maybe we could scare him away," suggested Lil.

"Why don't you sing another song, Angelica?" asked Phil. "That might scare him."

Angelica shot Phil a look.

"Well, then, there's only one thing left to do," said Tommy.

The babies exchanged knowing looks.

"You mean? . . ." asked Lil.

"Are you sure? . . ." asked Phil.

"What are you babies talking about?" demanded Angelica.

"Diapie attack!" said Tommy.

Angelica made a face. "Yuck! That's disgusting!"

The T. rex sniffed the air and then moved toward the babies. He stared down at them and opened his jaw wide to show his giant, sharp teeth. He took another step toward the babies. Just as he lunged at them he lost his balance and crashed down hard onto his back.

"He falled down!" said Kimi.

"But we weren't playing ring-around-a-nosey," said Lil.

"No time for small talk, babies! Let's get outta here!" cried Angelica.

Susie looked at the T. rex curiously. "Wait a minute. I think something's wrong with him."

"He's not moving," said Tommy. "Look! His foot is stuck in the rocks."

The tyrannosaurus's foot was wedged in a narrow crevice between two rocks. He tugged and tugged, but he was stuck.

"These dinosaurs aren't very smart," said Angelica. "They're always getting stuck in something. A rock, a tar pit! What's the matter with them?"

"Their brains aren't very big," explained Susie.

Angelica snorted. "I know some people like that."

"So do I," replied Susie.

The T. rex was frantically trying to

pull his foot from the crevice. He tried so hard that he slipped and fell again, hitting his head on a rock.

WHACK!

"Ow! That's gotta hurt," said Angelica.

The T. rex lay on the ground, very still. He had knocked himself out. He was alive and breathing, but unconscious.

"When he wakes up, he's gonna have a headache this big," said Angelica as she opened her arms wide. "Let's get outta here!"

"But he scared away that mad mommy dinosaur. I think we should help him," said Chuckie. The other babies looked at Chuckie in disbelief. "And he might be one of Reptar's cousins. He might even be the same dinosaur we saw in the mooseum."

"Yeah, if we don't save him, he might never make it to the mooseum," said Tommy. "And my daddy won't be able to

find out how to make the dancin'
dinosaur ride."

"Let's help him," said Susie.

Angelica let out a sigh. "What are we?
The dinosaur rescue squad?"

"How do we get him un-stucked?"
asked Lil.

"The rock is too big and heavy to
move," said Tommy. "But there's gotta be
a way."

Susie snapped her fingers. "I know!
We'll use leverage."

"What the heck is that?" asked
Angelica.

"It's when you wedge a stick or something underneath something that's too
heavy to move, and then you push on
the other side to lift it," said Susie. "I saw
it on the *Mr. Science* show."

She demonstrated by using a stick to
lift a small rock that was next to them.
She stuck the end of the stick under the

rock and then pushed down on the other end of the stick, and the rock lifted up.

Phil and Lil clapped their hands. "Like a seesaw!"

"We can use the tree that the T. rex knocked over," said Susie.

They dragged one end of the tree over to the rocks where the tyrannosaurus's foot was caught.

"Now we just push on this end and it will lift the rock up, and then the T. rex can get his foot out," said Susie.

"In case you haven't noticed, Susie, we're not the Olympic tree-lifting team," said Angelica.

"Our weight will lift it out," said Susie. "Trust me."

They stuck the tree carefully into the crevice and under the rock. Then they all jumped up and grabbed hold of the other end of the tree. Their feet dangled in the air as they hung on.

"It's not moving," said Tommy. "We don't weigh enough!"

"I knew I shoulda had that other Reptar bar for breakfast," said Phil.

Just then Spike jumped up onto the tree, and the log started to move. One end of the tree went down as the other end lifted the rock up, and it rolled off the T. rex's foot.

"Good job, Spike!" said Tommy.

"Okay, let's get out of here before the T. rex wakes up!" said Angelica.

Just then one of the T. rex's eyes opened.

"He's waking up!" cried Chuckie.

CHAPTER 12

The babies hid behind the rock they had rolled off the T. rex's foot. The T. rex looked around. He shook his giant head and then slowly stood up. The T. rex was still dazed as he started to walk away, and he didn't see the tree the babies had used to get his stuck foot out. It was balanced on the rock like a seesaw. He stepped on it with all his weight, and it flipped high up into the air and came crashing down on the T. rex's foot.

"ROARRRRRRRRRRRRR!"

The babies covered their ears.

"That is the clumsiest dinosaur I've ever seen!" said Angelica.

The T. rex started hopping back and forth, and the ground shook. He jumped in a circle, trying not to put his weight on his injured foot. He was hopping and jumping and spinning in a circle.

"Okay, guys, the toast is clear," said Tommy. "Let's get outta here while he's jumping around and not paying attention."

The babies ran away with Spike following close behind. Tommy turned around for one more look at the T. rex who was still hopping up and down. "I wish we coulda told him that someday he's gonna be in a mooseum and people would come to look at him and buy postcards with his picture on them."

Chuckie grinned. "Maybe all the dinosaurs we saw are gonna be famous someday."

They were almost back to the bushes when the sky went dark.

"It must be nighttime," said Kimi. "And we didn't even get to go to Buck E. Bee's for dinner."

Angelica looked at her pink Cynthia wristwatch and made a guess. "It's too early for nighttime."

"Then why is it getting so dark?" asked Chuckie.

"I don't know," said Susie, puzzled.

Angelica smiled. "So, miss Susie smarty-pants doesn't know *everything* does she?"

"Do you know why it's getting dark, Angelica?" asked Tommy.

"Well, um . . . ," stammered Angelica. She looked up and her face turned pale. "It's . . . it's . . . it's an asteroid! The asteroid is coming! It's gonna hit the Earth!"

CHAPTER 13

Angelica ran as fast as she could with the babies right behind her. She found the bushes they had crawled through earlier that afternoon and dove in. Chuckie ran through so fast he didn't even think about getting scratched by branches or bitten by bugs.

Angelica was the first one through the bushes into the backyard. "Help! Help! An asteroid is coming!"

Stu, who was working down in the basement, heard the noise and came running outside. "What is it, Angelica?"

Angelica pointed up in the sky. "Up there! An asteroid! It's gonna hit the

Earth and make us egg-stink like the dinosaurs!"

"What dinosaurs?" asked Stu.

Angelica pointed to the sky. "Up there! It's gonna block the sun and make it cold! And . . ."

Stu shaded his eyes with his hand and looked up. "That's just a big cloud blocking the sun. Don't worry, Angelica, nobody's going to be extinct. Now, I have to get back to work. I still haven't been able to figure out how to make that dancing dinosaur ride." He shook his head and went back inside.

Angelica looked up in the sky. It *was* just a cloud. A big, white, fluffy cloud. "Well, it *coulda* been an asteroid!" said Angelica.

Just then Susie's mother called from next door. "Susie, time for dinner!"

"See you later," said Susie as she skipped off toward her house. "Call me if you see any more asteroids!"

Angelica huffed and rolled her eyes.

Tommy turned to the others. "What do you want to do now?"

"EAT!" they all yelled.

The babies were eating big bowls of Reptar cereal in the den. Chuckie had his Reptar toy beside him and was making it growl. Spike was napping in the corner.

"Too bad we didn't see any dancing dinosaurs," said Chuckie. "We could've helped your daddy."

"He's pretty smart. I bet he'll figure it out," said Tommy.

Angelica walked into the room, holding something behind her back. "Okay, babies, I got a big surprise for you!"

"What is it?" asked Kimi.

Angelica held up a videotape. "*Return*

to the *Planet of the Dinosaurs, Part Two!*"

The babies cheered and clapped their hands.

"Let's see it!" said Tommy.

"Keep your diapers on! I gots to re-whine it first," said Angelica as she pushed some buttons on the VCR.

"I hope it gots a T. rex in it," said Tommy. "Remember when that T. rex hurt his foot and jumped up and down?"

"Yeah, that was kinda funny now that I'm not scareded anymore," said Chuckie.

"Like this?" said Tommy, getting up and jumping around like the T. rex.

Chuckie laughed. "You look just like him!"

"Come on, do it with me! It's fun!" cried Tommy.

The babies jumped up and started imitating the T. rex. They waved their hands in the air and hopped up and down in a circle.

"Shake your booties!" cried Lil.

"Sell it, sister!" shouted Phil.

"Let me hear you say 'roar'!" yelled Tommy.

"ROAR!"

"I can't hear you!"

"ROAR! ROAR!"

Clump! Clump! Clump! went their feet on the floor.

Down in the basement Stu heard the racket and ran upstairs. "What's all the ruckus? I can't work with all this noise. I'm still trying to figure out how to make those dang dinosaurs dance. . . ."

Stu saw the babies hopping up and down and roaring like the T. rex. A big smile spread across his face. "That's it! *That's* the way a dinosaur would dance! I've got to call Paris! Thanks, kids!" As he ran back downstairs he called out, "We can go to Buck E. Bee's when I finish my phone call!"

Tommy high-fived Chuckie. "I guess it's been a pretty good day," he said.

"Hey, zip your lips! It's time for the movie," said Angelica.

"Is it scary?" asked Chuckie. "I don't like scary movies."

"I don't think it'll scare you, Chuckie," said Tommy. "You wasn't even afraid of that T. rex!"

"That's right. I wasn't," said Chuckie with a big smile. "But if I do get scareded, I can just cover my eyes."

"Okay, it's showtime!" said Angelica as she pressed the PLAY button on the VCR. "And as a special treat, I will be singing along with all the songs."

Tommy whispered to Chuckie, "You better cover your ears, too!"

About the Author

Steven Banks is a writer, actor, and musician. He has written scripts for *CatDog, Fairly Oddparents, and Jimmy Neutron: Boy Genius.* Steven has also written *SpongeBob Squarepants, Rocket Power, and CatDog* books. He had his own TV show called *The Steven Banks Show* on PBS and a special on Showtime called *Home Entertainment Center.* When he was a kid, Steven loved to read (and still does!) and had a great collection of toy dinosaurs that he wishes he still had!